THE POCKET

Mark Twain

Quizzes & Puzzles

Published in 2025
by Gemini Books
Part of Gemini Books Group

Based in Woodbridge and London
Marine House, Tide Mill Way
Woodbridge, Suffolk IP12 1AP
United Kingdom

www.geminibooks.com

Cover image: Shutterstock/T. Gorhum

ISBN 978-1-80247-273-8

A CIP catalogue record for this book is available from the British Library.
from the British Library.

Printed in China

10 9 8 7 6 5 4 3 2 1

FSC
www.fsc.org
MIX
Paper | Supporting responsible forestry
FSC® C020056

THE POCKET

Mark Twain

Quizzes & Puzzles

G:

Contents

INTRODUCTION

Drawing on *The Adventures of Tom Sawyer*, its sequel, *Adventures of Huckleberry Finn* and Mark Twain's other books, the ingenious quizzes and puzzles in this fun collection will test your memory of the writer described by Nobel laureate William Faulkner as 'the father of American literature'.

Born Samuel Langhorne Clemens in 1835, in Florida, Missouri, Mark Twain, as a result of his father's death, had to leave school at the age of twelve to earn his living. He worked as an apprentice to a printer, prospected – unsuccessfully – for gold, then left for South America to make his fortune.

All the answers to the puzzles are to be found in the pages of Twain's best known published work. The name games require the names of characters to be given to reveal a final name, while each crossword puzzle relies on quotations from one of Twain's works. The wordsearch puzzles explore various themes in his writing.

All the answers are given at the back of the book, but elusive answers will hopefully encourage you to reread *Adventures of Huckleberry Finn* – of which Hemingway said, 'All Modern American literature comes from [this] one book' – and all Twain's other works.

E·W·Kemble
·1884·

MARK TWAIN

Known as a humourist, journalist, novelist and lecturer, Mark Twain was born Samuel Langhorne Clemens on 30 November 1835 in Florida, Missouri, during the appearance of Halley's Comet. His father, a lawyer, died when he was twelve years old, causing Clemens to leave school to train as an apprentice printer on a local newspaper. By the age of eighteen, he was working on several newspapers in New York and Philadelphia. The young Sam Clemens had fantasised about travel and, following a boat trip in New Orleans, he decided to train as a riverboat pilot on the Mississippi River, a job he held for four years. The people and towns he encountered along the river became the basis for the places and characters in his most famous books, *The Adventures of Tom Sawyer* and *Adventures of Huckleberry Finn*.

When the Civil War broke out in 1861, river transportation stopped and Clemens joined the Confederate militia. It wasn't for long. Within two weeks, his brother had convinced him to leave and head west to California on a joint gold-mining adventure. The trip later became the inspiration for his book *Roughing It*. The mining proved unsuccessful and Clemens ended up writing for the Nevada newspaper the *Territorial Enterprise*, where he first used the name Mark Twain. The name came from his steamboat days, when the measure of the depth of the water was called by a crewman, 'mark twain' meant 'two fathoms'. Twain's writing career, as we know it, really began when he was working as a journalist in San Francisco. Inspired by a tale he heard in a bar, in 1865 he wrote and published a short story, *The Celebrated Jumping Frog of Calaveras County*. It gained him national attention and Twain devoted the rest of his life to writing.

In 1870, he married Olivia Langdon. The couple met after Twain became friends with her brother Charles, during a steamship tour of Europe a few years earlier. Twain, his wife and their first child Langdon Clemens moved to Hartford, Connecticut in 1871, where Twain's most famous books were written.

A year later, their daughter Susy was born, but, sadly, Langdon died aged two from diphtheria.

The Clemens went on to have two more daughters, Clara, born in 1874, and Jean, in 1880.

Unfortunately, unwise investments in new inventions led to bankruptcy, and caused the family to move to Europe, where Twain was forced to set out on a worldwide lecture tour, so he could repay debts. Tragedy struck in 1896 when Susy Clemens died from meningitis at the age of twenty-four, while on a visit to the Hartford home. Unable to bear being in the place of her death, the Clemens never lived in Hartford again.

The family returned to the USA from Europe in 1900, with their finances restored, and Twain declared himself an anti-imperialist; from 1901 until his death, he served as vice president of the Anti-Imperialist League. His dark, anti-government rhetoric almost led to more financial trouble, because magazines and publishers refused to accept his writing, fearing his marketable reputation would be ruined. As a result, a lot of Twain's work from that period was published posthumously.

In 1903, while living in New York City, Olivia fell ill, and the couple went to live in Italy, where Olivia died a year later. After her death, Twain returned to the USA, eventually settling in Redding, Connecticut. Jean Clemens, their youngest daughter, died from an epileptic seizure in 1909. Four months later, on 21 April 1910, Mark Twain died aged seventy-four, coincidentally during the year of the next appearance of Halley's Comet. He was survived by only one of his four children, Clara Clemens.

Mark Twain

Samuel Clemens (Mark Twain), aged fifteen,
holding metal type that spells out his first name.

Quizzes & Puzzles

Wordsearch 1
Characters in *Adventures of Huckleberry Finn*

Concealed in the grid are the names of fifteen characters in *Adventures of Huckleberry Finn*. They may read horizontally, vertically or diagonally, backwards or forwards, and letters may be used more than once, or not at all. Circle the answers on the grid on the facing page and list them in the space below.

A	S	B	A	M	Y	L	A	W	R	E	N	C	E	P
C	D	I	E	F	T	O	M	S	A	W	Y	E	R	U
G	H	I	L	J	K	L	M	N	O	L	P	R	Q	D
J	O	E	H	A	R	P	E	R	L	R	E	S	T	D
U	V	W	X	Y	S	Z	V	O	K	Y	L	G	S	N
C	J	E	N	S	L	P	P	T	W	P	F	H	D	H
B	B	E	C	K	Y	T	H	A	T	C	H	E	R	E
K	V	F	R	E	N	S	S	E	A	K	W	B	R	A
J	X	K	Q	U	V	D	I	F	L	Y	K	U	O	D
W	H	Z	A	G	I	J	A	F	Q	P	S	A	B	W
T	P	A	P	S	F	I	N	N	J	R	S	Z	I	I
R	V	C	P	A	D	K	B	J	Q	J	T	L	N	L
U	W	X	C	O	M	R	D	O	B	B	I	N	S	S
M	U	F	F	P	O	T	T	E	R	Q	U	M	O	O
H	U	C	K	L	E	B	E	R	R	Y	F	I	N	N

Name Game I

Name the novel and fill the character names into the grid on the facing page. The name of a further character from the same novel will appear, reading down. A full point marks the division between two parts of any character's name.

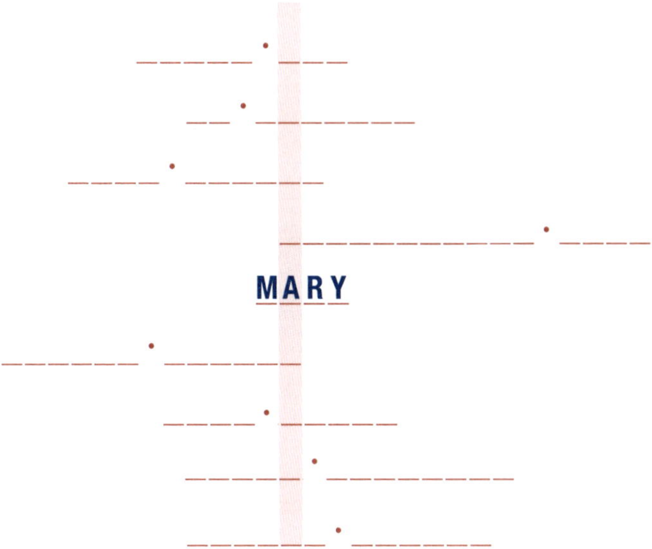
MARY

Picture Puzzle 1

Guess which character or characters are shown in the picture below. To make the puzzle a little bit harder, the name of the novel has not been given, but all answers can be found at the back of the book.

Name the characters in the illustration below.

....

....

....

First to Last

Put the following Mark Twain novels in the order in which they were written.

1 *Adventures of Huckleberry Finn*

2 *The Annotated Huckleberry Finn*

3 *The Adventures of Tom Sawyer*

4 *Tom Sawyer, Detective*

5 *Tom Sawyer Abroad*

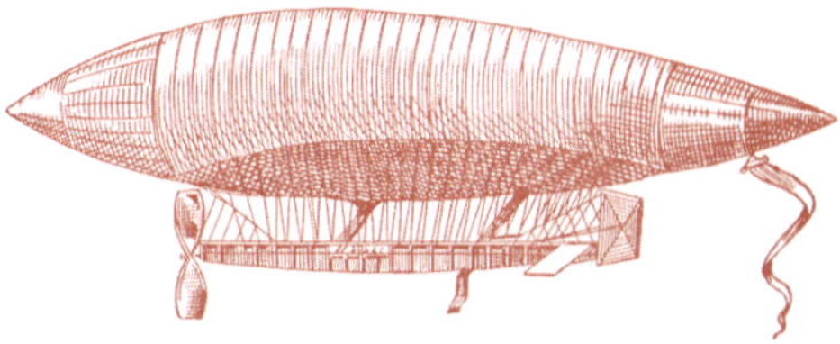

The Adventures of Tom Sawyer (1876)

Tom Sawyer lives with his Aunt Polly and half-brother Sid on the banks of the Mississippi. One day, he skips school and gets into a fight. His punishment is to whitewash a fence, but he tricks other boys into doing the work by persuading them that it is a great honour.

Supposedly engaged to Amy Lawrence, he falls in love with Becky Thatcher and gets engaged to her too. But Becky hears of his previous engagement and backs off.

Feeling humiliated, Tom plans to run away. He meets Huckleberry (Huck) Finn, a poor, feral boy. While at the graveyard, where they have met to test a cure for warts involving a dead cat, the boys witness a murder. Injun Joe kills Dr Robinson, then frames drunken Muff Potter. Afraid of telling anyone, the boys swear an oath of silence.

Tom runs away to Jackson's Island with Huck and another boy, Joe Harper. It dawns on them that they are the three boys, presumed drowned, that a search party is looking for. They don't reveal their identities until their memorial 'funerals', when they walk into the church to surprise their mourners.

Tom persists with Becky, but without much success. At Muff Potter's trial, Tom testifies that Muff is innocent. Injun Joe escapes, but Tom's courage has reignited Becky's interest. They go to explore some caves, where they find Injun Joe hiding. The people of the town block the cave, where Injun Joe dies. Later, Tom and Huck return to the caves and discover a box of gold that belonged to Injun Joe. Tom finds happiness with Becky, while Huck becomes respectable through having an 'inheritance', also being adopted.

Crossword 1 Characters in *Adventures of Huckleberry Finn*

Across

4 Character who takes care of Huck at the beginning of the novel (12)

6 Huck's abusive and alcoholic father (3)

9 What is the name of the character who pretends to be a deaf mute boy? (7)

12 This character was shot in the leg during a gunfight (15)

13 Who helps Jim escape from captivity? (9)

Down

1 What is the name of the drunk who tries to steal Huck's money? (5)

2 Huck's best friend and partner in crime (9)

3 Wealthy and respected citizen in the town who wants to help Huck (13)

5 What is the name of the family that takes Huck in and tries to educate him? (12)

7 Huck's strict guardian (9)

8 Huck's companion (3)

10 Con artist who travels with the Dauphin (4)

11 Protagonist and narrator of the story (4)

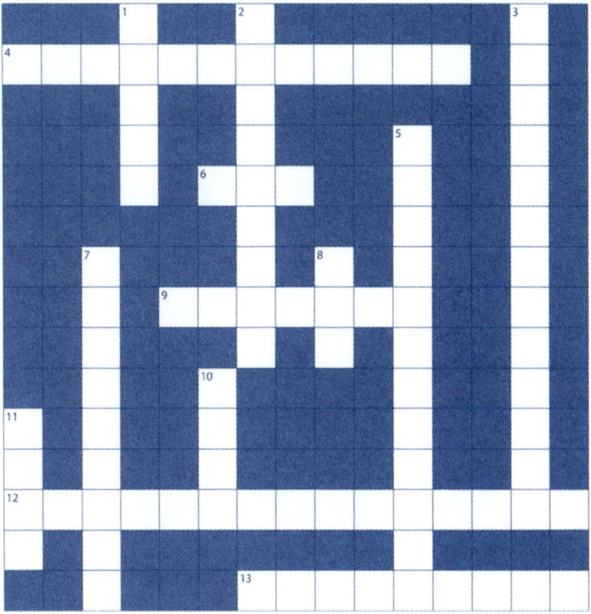

Cryptogram 1
Puddn'head Wilson's Calendar

In *The Tragedy of Puddn'head Wilson*, each chapter begins with an aphorism from 'Pudd'nhead Wilson's Calendar' – sayings collected by David Wilson, the narrator. Below is a cryptogram of one of those sayings. Each letter in the phrase has been replaced with a random number. See if you can unravel it.

A	B	C	D	E	F	G	H	I	J	K	L	M
16	11						18					22

N	O	P	Q	R	S	T	U	V	W	X	Y	Z
					23	24			6		25	

M	A	_		M	A	Y		H	A	_	_
22	16	25		22	16	5		18	16	13	26

_	_		B	A	_		H	A	B	_	T	S
25	4		11	16	10		18	16	11	1	24	23

A	_	_		H	A	_	_		W	_	_	S	_
16	25	10		18	16	13	26		6	4	15	23	26

Quiz 1
Relations in Mark Twain's Novels

Family (or lack of it), is a theme in Mark Twain's writing. Answer the following questions regarding who is related to whom. What were the first names of the following characters?

1 Tom Sawyer's half-brother ....

2 Huckleberry Finn's father ....

3 Aunt Polly's sister ....

4 Becky Thatcher's father ....

5 Tom Driscoll's father ....

6 Valet de Chambre (Chambers)'s mother ....

7 Colonel Mulberry Sellers's daughter ....

8 The twin brother of Angelo Capello ....

9 Sally Phelps's husband ....

10 Edward Tudor's father ....

True or False?

Mark Twain is famous for his many quotations. However, many are incorrectly attributed to him. Which of the following quotations cannot be attributed to Mark Twain?

1 a. 'If you wish to inflict a heartless and malignant punishment upon a young person, pledge him to keep a journal a year.'
b. 'Never put off until tomorrow what you can do today.'
c. 'When you catch an adjective, kill it.'
d. 'An honest man in politics shines more there than he would elsewhere.'

2 a. 'An author values a compliment even when it comes from a source of doubtful competency.'
b. 'Twenty years from now you will be more disappointed by the things you didn't do than by the ones you did do.'
c. 'Whenever you find yourself on the side of the majority, it is time to reform (or pause and reflect).'
d. 'There is probably no pleasure equal to the pleasure of climbing a dangerous Alp; but it is a pleasure which is confined strictly to people who can find pleasure in it.'

3 a. 'It is better to keep your mouth shut and appear stupid than to open it and remove all doubt.'

b. 'Familiarity breeds contempt – and children.'

c. 'A classic ... something that everybody wants to have read and nobody wants to read.'

d. 'Concerning the difference between man and the jackass: some observers hold that there isn't any. But this wrongs the jackass.'

4 a. 'If I had more time, I would have written a shorter letter.'

b. 'Get a bicycle. You will not regret it. If you live.'

c. 'If everybody was satisfied with himself there would be no heroes.'

d. 'That desire which is in us all to better other people's condition by having them think as we think.'

5 a. 'Nothing so needs reforming as other people's habits.'

b. 'Arguments are unsafe with wives, because they examine them; but they do not examine compliments.'

c. 'Go to Heaven for the climate, Hell for the company.'

d. 'You should never do anything wicked and lay it on your brother, when it is just as convenient to lay it on some other boy.'

Wordsearch 2
Places in *A Tramp Abroad*

Concealed in the grid on the facing page are the names of fourteen places named in *A Tramp Abroad*. The names may read horizontally, vertically or diagonally, backwards or forwards, and letters may be used more than once, or not at all. Circle the answers on the grid and list them in the space below.

A	B	C	D	E	F	G	G	H	I	J	K	E	L	M
N	O	P	Z	Q	R	S	T	E	U	V	C	T	W	X
B	A	D	E	N	B	A	D	E	N	I	S	Y	Z	C
I	B	D	R	L	U	C	E	R	N	E	K	K	I	Q
T	B	L	M	R	K	Z	Q	E	R	N	V	M	N	C
A	O	I	A	Q	H	Y	V	O	Y	N	H	A	T	I
O	O	Z	T	G	W	K	F	G	G	T	Q	N	E	F
X	E	Y	T	F	D	K	R	J	X	E	A	N	R	W
J	F	B	N	W	C	X	A	I	V	L	R	H	L	R
K	E	K	O	A	W	B	N	V	I	B	U	E	A	U
P	G	D	L	S	X	O	C	M	W	W	D	I	K	J
J	K	B	E	P	M	U	E	R	X	R	O	M	E	D
N	E	C	K	A	R	R	I	V	E	R	N	A	N	D
J	A	S	H	E	I	D	E	L	B	E	R	G	O	V
O	G	C	R	A	C	D	E	J	O	O	P	F	M	E

Name Game 2

Name the novel and fill the character names into the grid on the facing page. The name of a further character from the same novel will appear, reading down. A full point marks the division between two parts of any character's name.

TOM · CANTY

Picture Puzzle 2

Name the characters in the illustration below.

....

....

....

....

'A classic ... something that everybody wants to have read and nobody wants to read.'

Mark Twain, in a speech on the disappearance of literature

Adventures of Huckleberry Finn (1884)

Huckleberry (Huck) Finn is a young boy who has become rich through his adventures with Tom Sawyer. He has been adopted by Widow Douglas and her sister Miss Watson, who are trying to teach him manners and religion, but Huck sneaks out of the house at night to join Tom and his gang.

When Huck's drunken, abusive father Pap Finn returns, he berates Huck for trying to better himself and demands that he quit school. When Huck refuses, Pap kidnaps him and takes him to a small cabin in Illinois. Huck escapes and sets sail down the Mississippi, returning to Jackson's island where he finds Jim, Miss Watson's slave, who has run away.

They hear that men are coming to search for Jim, so the two escape on a raft. Jim wants to reach Illinois, where he can travel up the Ohio River to the free states.

Huck and Jim encounter many characters on their journey. Two men known as The Duke and The King commandeer the raft, forcing Huck and Jim to visit various towns as they carry out confidence scams. In one town, The Duke and The King plan to pose as English brothers in order to steal an inheritance, but their plan fails when the real brothers turn up. The ensuing chaos allows Huck and Jim to escape, but the confidence tricksters soon catch up with them.

They betray Huck and Jim by selling Jim back into slavery. When Huck discovers that Jim is being kept captive by Tom Sawyer's aunt and uncle, Silas and Sally Phelps, he poses as Tom. When the real Tom turns up, Tom has to pose as his own brother Sid. The boys concoct various complicated plans to free Jim, mostly based on stories Tom has read. When they do escape, Tom is shot in the leg and, unwilling to leave the injured Tom, Jim is recaptured. Tom reveals Jim's plan to get to freedom to his aunt and uncle.

While Huck has been away, Miss Watson has died, freeing Jim in her will. We learn that Tom has known this all along and was simply wanting to take part in Huck and Jim's adventure. Jim is freed and Huck starts planning his next adventure.

Crossword 2
The Life of Mark Twain

Across

1 Who was the only person to film Mark Twain? (13)

3 What river was known as the Big Muddy? (11)

9 What was Mark Twain's wife called? (6)

10 How many feet is two fathoms (the 'twain' from where Mark Twain got his name)? (6)

11 What job did Twain attempt, after fleeing San Francisco because he owed money? (5)

12 What animal featured in Mark Twain's short story that his first published fiction? (4)

13 How many grandchildren did Mark Twain have? (3)

14 How many years did it take Mark Twain to write *Adventures of Huckleberry Finn*? (5)

Down

1 What was the real name of the boy Twain based Huckleberry Finn on? (14)

2 What cosmic phenomenon happened both in the year of Twain's birth and his death? (11)

4 What was Mark Twain's astrological star sign? (11)

5 What colour suit was Mark Twain famous for wearing? (5)

6 What type of machine did he invest in that caused him to go bankrupt? (10)

7 How many children did Mark Twain have? (4)

8 What was Mark Twain's favourite animal? (3)

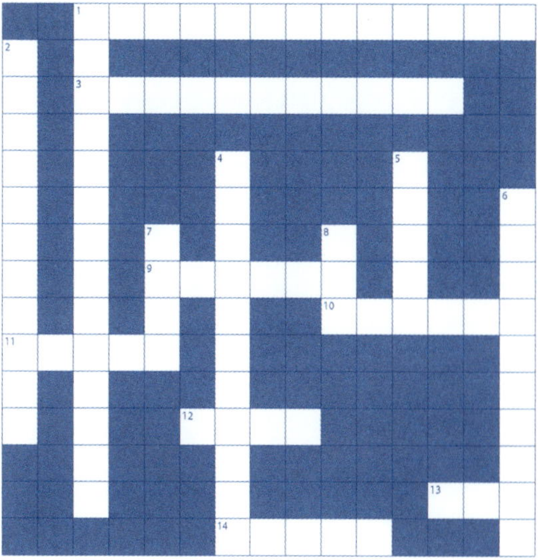

Cryptogram 2
Puddn'head Wilson's Calendar

In *The Tragedy of Puddn'head Wilson*, each chapter begins with an aphorism from 'Pudd'nhead Wilson's Calendar' – sayings collected by David Wilson, the narrator. Below is a cryptogram of one of those sayings. Each letter in the phrase has been replaced with a random number. See if you can unravel it.

A	B	C	D	E	F	G	H	I	J	K	L	M
14				24	3							

N	O	P	Q	R	S	T	U	V	W	X	Y	Z
	8						6	19	12			

W		E			A							O	U		
12	1	24	15		14	15	18	10	4		2	8	6	15	23

F	O	U			W		E			V	E		
3	8	6	10		12	1	24	15		19	24	10	4

A							W	E	A	
14	15	18	10	4		13	12	24	14	10

Quiz 2
Places in the Novels of Mark Twain

Travel, odysseys, pilgrimages and adventures feature in all Mark Twain's books. Answer the following about the places associated with the characters.

1. Where did Tom Sawyer live?
2. Where did Tom Canty first see Edward, Prince of Wales?
3. Where did David 'Pudd'nhead' Wilson live?
4. Where did Tom Canty's family live?
5. Where do Huck, Tom and Joe Harper run away to?
6. Where does Hank Morgan find himself after a blow to the head?
7. Where does Berkeley Rossmore live?
8. Where does Tom Driscoll attend college?
9. On which river does Roxy get a job on a boat?
10. Where do Tom Sawyer, Huck Finn and Jim travel to in a hot air balloon?

Wordsearch 3
Food in *A Tramp Abroad*

Concealed in the grid on the facing page are the names of eighteen foods named in *A Tramp Abroad*. The words may read horizontally, vertically or diagonally, backwards or forwards, and letters may be used more than once, or not at all. Circle the answers on the grid and list them in the space below.

A	B	B	C	D	C	L	A	M	S	E	F	G	T	H
I	J	L	K	L	M	N	R	A	D	I	S	H	E	S
O	O	A	P	Q	C	A	C	P	R	S	T	U	R	H
V	Y	C	W	X	R	P	R	L	Y	Z	I	S	R	E
Q	S	K	R	S	A	P	O	E	Y	S	C	N	A	E
L	T	B	P	A	N	L	A	S	O	O	W	W	P	P
T	E	A	Q	P	B	E	K	Y	R	K	N	O	I	S
J	R	S	T	O	E	S	E	R	U	I	W	O	N	H
X	S	S	R	S	R	K	R	U	T	V	M	D	G	E
K	M	P	O	S	R	E	S	P	Y	S	H	C	I	A
O	M	V	U	U	I	C	S	S	D	Q	B	O	V	D
Z	J	K	T	M	E	B	E	Q	N	L	F	C	P	L
V	X	W	L	L	S	R	A	C	H	I	C	K	E	N
V	K	P	V	O	K	B	U	C	K	W	H	E	A	T
P	A	R	T	R	I	D	G	E	S	C	F	O	K	Q

Name Game 3

Name the novel and fill the character names into the grid on the facing page. The name of a further character from the same novel will appear, reading down. A full point marks the division between two parts of any character's name.

_ _ _ . _ _ _ _ _ _

_ _ _ . _ _ _ _

_ _ _ _ . _ _ _ _ _ _ _

_ _ _ . _ _ _ _ _ _

_ _ _ . _ _ _ _ _ _

_ _ _ _ . _ _ _ _ _ _ _ _ _ _ _

DR. ROBINSON

_ _ _ _ _ _ _ _ _ _ _ . _ _ _ _

_ _ _ _ _ . _ _ _ _ _ _ _ _

_ _ _ _ _ . _ _ _ _ _

_ _ _ _ _ . _ _ _ _ _ _

_ _ _ _ _ _ _ . _ _ _ _ _ _ _ _

Picture Puzzle 3

Name the characters in the illustration below.

....

....

....

....

'God Almighty made us all, and some He gives eyes that's blind, and some He gives eyes that can see, and I reckon it ain't none of our lookout what He done it for; it's all right, or He'd 'a' fixed it some other way.'

Tom Sawyer, Detective

Tom Sawyer Abroad (1894)

Tom, Huckleberry Finn and Jim are kidnapped by an inventor called The Professor, who is determined to fly around the world in a hot air balloon. They fly high enough to see that the Earth is round, which Huck had always doubted, and far enough to realise that there are different time zones, something that Jim had always worried about. One night, the professor, drunk, falls over the side of the balloon during a violent storm and is killed.

Tom, Huck and Jim continue their travels across the world without him. They fly over England, and land in Africa where they almost get eaten by lions. In the Sahara Desert they see a caravan of camels being attacked by bandits. One of the bandits had stolen a child, so the boys use the balloon to knock him off his camel and reunite the child with its mother. They find and follow a new caravan of camels, this one being buried by a giant sandstorm, as are they in their balloon basket, up to their necks.

They travel on, having adventures among the pyramids in Egypt and in the Holy Land. On Mount Sinai, Tom's corncob pipe breaks and he refuses any pipe other than a corncob one. He sends Huck and Jim home in the balloon to fetch another one, but they come back telling him that Aunt

Polly wouldn't give them one and they had to go home. At this, they reluctantly head back to Missouri.

Crossword 3
The Adventures of Tom Sawyer

Across

2 What does Tom see while he is temporarily dead in the cave? (6)

4 What game do Tom and his friends play along the river? (7)

6 The location of the treasure hunt (4)

7 Who was accused of murder and defended by Tom and Huck? (7)

9 The key ingredient in Becky's misspelled note (5)

10 What colour was both Becky and Huck's hair? (3)

13 The location where Tom and Becky get lost (10)

14 Tom's crush and love interest (5)

15 What is Becky's nickname for Tom? (6)

Down

1 Where does Tom hide in the graveyard during the funeral procession? (7)

3 Location where Tom and Huck witness a terrifying scene and swear to secrecy about it (9)

5 Nickname given to Tom by his friends (6)

8 What does Tom trick his friends into helping him whitewash instead of doing it himself? (5)

10 Means of transportation along the Mississippi River (4)

11 What Joe Harper has when Tom meets him in the woods at midnight (4)

12 What type of farmers do Tom and Huck pretend to be? (4)

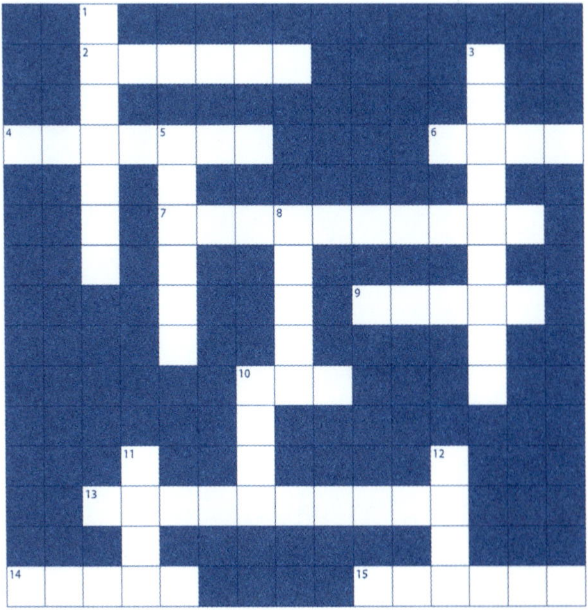

Cryptogram 3
Puddn'head Wilson's Calendar

In *The Tragedy of Puddn'head Wilson*, each chapter begins with an aphorism from 'Pudd'nhead Wilson's Calendar' – sayings collected by David Wilson, the narrator. Below is a cryptogram of one of those sayings. Each letter in the phrase has been replaced with a random number. See if you can unravel it.

A	B	C	D	E	F	G	H	I	J	K	L	M
				3						9	14	

N	O	P	Q	R	S	T	U	V	W	X	Y	Z
20	5				15				16			

W		E	N			L	L		L			K
16	6	3	20		2	14	14		14	23	11	9

	E			N	S						O	E	S		N	O	
1	3	4	2	20	15		2	12		26	5	3	15		20	5	12

	O		E			N		S				N	K	L	E	S
11	5	17	23		2	20		15	10	21	2	20	9	14	3	15

					N		S		O	W	E		S
1	23	12		2	20		15	6	5	16	3	21	15

Quiz 3
Crime in Mark Twain's Novels

Theft, murder, subterfuge, sabotage and piracy are all themes in Mark Twain's books. Answer the following questions about crime.

1. What do Huck and Tom find in the cave?
2. Who killed Dr Robinson?
3. How do The King and The Duke try to gain the estate of a Peter Wilks?
4. What crime does Tom Sawyer try to initiate with a gang of other boys?
5. How does Huckleberry Finn fake his own death?
6. How was Pap Finn killed?
7. Who is killed in the gunfight between the Grangerfords and the Shepherdsons?
8. Where does Huck drop the stolen money he took back from the King and Duke?
9. Who is framed for the murder of Dr Robinson?
10. What crime did Dr Robinson, Muff Potter and Injun Joe commit?

Wordsearch 4
Fish and Amphibians in the Writing of Mark Twain

Concealed in the grid on the facing page are the names of seventeen fish and amphibians named in Mark Twain's writing. The words may read horizontally, vertically or diagonally, backwards or forwards, and letters may be used more than once, or not at all. Circle the answers on the grid and list them in the space below.

M	U	S	K	E	L	L	U	N	G	E	A	B	B	C
D	E	F	G	H	I	J	K	L	T	M	N	L	O	P
Q	R	S	T	S	U	W	V	U	W	X	Y	U	Z	P
L	L	D	M	Z	R	A	O	G	U	W	K	E	S	A
B	B	A	R	N	T	R	M	H	B	H	Z	G	T	D
W	L	S	W	S	T	M	E	G	S	O	B	I	U	D
C	A	U	F	H	A	O	X	I	V	T	U	L	R	L
C	B	L	E	O	I	U	F	P	X	U	L	L	G	E
L	N	Y	L	B	E	T	G	O	C	R	L	S	E	F
E	T	H	D	E	A	H	E	E	C	T	F	T	O	I
E	Y	M	P	C	Y	S	Y	B	R	L	R	C	N	S
C	R	A	P	P	I	E	S	B	A	E	O	T	T	H
P	R	C	O	M	U	S	S	E	L	S	G	Z	G	N
I	X	G	R	E	E	N	F	R	O	G	S	P	S	E
Z	Z	N	S	J	F	K	C	H	R	P	B	M	J	H

Picture Puzzle 4

Name the characters in the illustration below.

....

....

'Learning can only happen when a child is interested. If he's not interested, it's like throwing marshmallows at his head and calling it eating.'

Mark Twain

Tom Sawyer, Detective (1896)

Jake Dunlap is a burglar who has escaped from prison and is presumed dead. His brother, Brace Dunlap is trying to force Tom's Uncle Silas's daughter, Benny, to marry him and has made him take on Jake's violent twin brother, Jupiter, as a labourer. The Dunlaps are wealthier and more influential than the Phelps and Silas dislikes them intensely. Uncle Silas, a clergyman as well as a farmer, is repeatedly angered by Jupiter and they frequently argue, causing the people of the town to question his suitability as a church leader.

During a steamboat trip from Missouri to Arkansas, to visit Tom's distressed uncle and family, Tom and Huck meet Jake. He is currently on the run from other thieves from whom he has stolen diamonds. The boys take Jake to the farm belonging to Tom's Uncle Silas. Unfortunately, someone on board the steamboat overhears their plan and tips off Jake's old crime partners.

When Jupiter Dunlap disappears, Tom's Uncle Silas is charged with his murder. There is, however, no body. Tom, with the help of Huck takes on the role of detective and lawyer, hoping to solve the mystery and recover the diamonds.

Crossword 4
Mark Twain's Humour

Across

4 Be ... to your superiors, if you have any. (10)

5 If you don't read the newspaper, you're uninformed. If you read the newspaper, you're ... (11)

7 The funniest things are the ... (9)

10 When you fish for love, bait with your ..., not your brain. (5)

12 Let us live so that when we come to die even the ... will be sorry. (10)

13 Do the right thing. It will gratify some people and ... the rest. (8)

Down

1 It ain't those parts of the ... that I can't understand that bother me, it is the parts that I do understand. (5)

2 I love a drink, but I never encouraged ... by harping on its alleged funny side. (11)

3 Against the assault of laughter, nothing can ... (5)

6 Everything human is pathetic. The secret source of humour itself is not joy but ... There is no humour in heaven. (6)

8 Politicians and ... must be changed often, and for the same reason. (7)

9 The humorous story is told gravely; the teller does his best to ... the fact that he even dimly suspects that there is anything funny about it. (7)

11 What, sir, would the people of the earth be without ...? They would be scarce, sir, almighty scarce. (5)

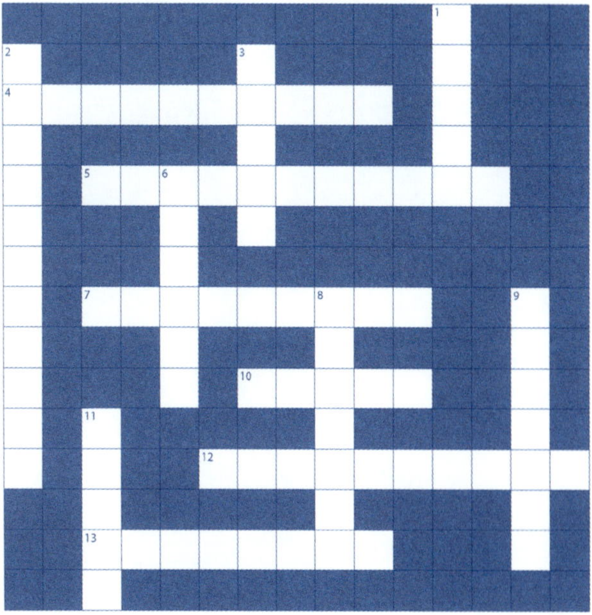

Cryptogram 4
Puddn'head Wilson's Calendar

In *The Tragedy of Puddn'head Wilson*, each chapter begins with an aphorism from 'Pudd'nhead Wilson's Calendar' – sayings collected by David Wilson, the narrator. Below is a cryptogram of one of those sayings. Each letter in the phrase has been replaced with a random number. See if you can unravel it.

A	B	C	D	E	F	G	H	I	J	K	L	M
6		22		1	7	23						

N	O	P	Q	R	S	T	U	V	W	X	Y	Z
				21	24							

C			R	A	G	E			S
22	14	10	21	6	23	1		11	24

R	E	S		S		A		C	E					F	E	A	R
21	1	24	11	24	25	6	13	22	1		25	14		7	1	6	21

	A	S		E	R				F		F	E	A	R				
18	6	24	25	1	21	3		14	7		7	1	6	21		13	14	25

A		S	E		C	E			F		F	E	A	R
6	15	24	1	13	22	1		14	7		7	1	6	21

Quiz 4
Dialect in the Novels of Mark Twain

In *Adventures of Huckleberry Finn*, Mark Twain used the common dialect of the time. Much of it can be hard to decipher. What is the meaning of the following words?

1 Gwyne

2 Sugar hogshead

3 Sap-head

4 Hifalut'n

5 Nabob

6 Consekens

7 Grifters

8 Yellocution

9 Smouch

10 Juice-harp

11 Nonnamous

12 The Tooleries

13 Brer

Wordsearch 5
Themes

Concealed in the grid on the facing page are twelve themes in *Adventures of Huckleberry Finn*. The words may read horizontally, vertically or diagonally, backwards or forwards, and letters may be used more than once, or not at all. Circle the answers on the grid and list them in the space below.

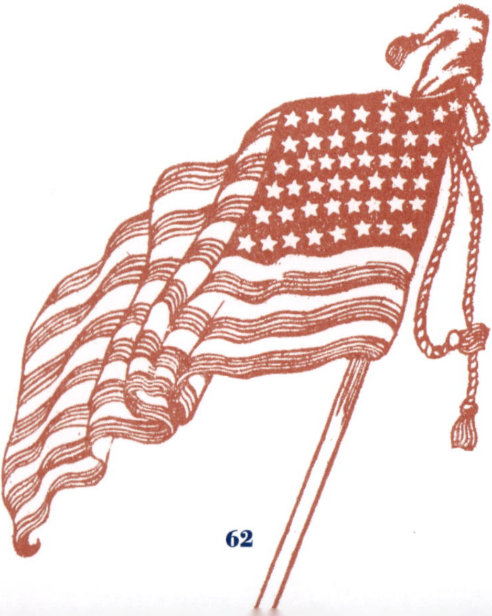

M	O	R	A	L	I	T	Y	A	L	B	C	D	E	F
G	O	H	I	J	K	L	M	E	N	O	P	Q	H	R
S	T	N	U	V	W	X	V	Y	Z	A	I	Q	Y	X
R	J	R	E	F	L	A	S	L	N	C	F	N	P	F
F	P	Q	X	Y	R	A	W	O	N	I	B	A	O	R
R	Q	S	J	T	J	I	U	E	C	V	X	S	C	E
Q	Z	S	D	W	A	E	E	J	A	I	A	W	R	E
L	H	A	Q	L	D	D	D	N	F	L	E	O	I	D
S	N	M	L	H	C	J	V	U	D	I	T	T	S	O
S	O	M	A	X	J	Q	U	E	C	S	G	H	Y	M
O	X	L	Y	U	M	V	C	S	N	A	H	R	W	P
T	M	T	M	K	O	O	K	D	T	T	T	I	R	W
H	M	L	O	H	E	Q	V	L	Q	I	U	I	P	F
E	T	D	F	M	J	T	T	Q	V	O	C	R	O	Q
V	N	Q	Y	B	C	L	J	Z	M	N	P	E	E	N

Picture Puzzle 5

Name the characters in the illustration below.

....

....

....

....

....

'They said they would rather be outlaws a year in Sherwood Forest than President of the United States forever.'

The Adventures of Tom Sawyer

The Prince and the Pauper (1881)

Tom Canty lives in Offal Court, in one of London's poorest areas. His father forces him to go out begging and beats him if he comes home empty-handed. A local priest takes pity on the boy and educates him, while telling him tales about the nobility.

Tom Canty and Edward Tudor, Prince of Wales and son of Henry VIII, look uncannily like one another. One day, Edward encounters Tom at the gates of the palace and talks to him. Tom is fascinated by the luxury that Edward enjoys; and Edward, by Tom's freedom. They agree to swap clothes, but the palace guards then assume that Edward is a poor boy so they throw him out. When Edward protests that he is the King's son, he is mocked and chased away. He is found by Tom's father, who drags him home. Meanwhile, Tom is initially amused by the luxury surrounding him, but starts to worry about what will happen if he is found out. Lady Jane Grey is confused by the changed behaviour of 'the prince' and word spreads that he has gone mad.

Meanwhile, John Canty tries to earn money from the real Edward Tudor's 'delusion' that he is the Prince of Wales. When Canty learns that a man he struck has died, they have to flee, and Edward escapes.

He tries to get in to a dinner at the Guildhall, but is stopped. Miles Hendon comes to his defence. In Hendon's rooms, the prince acts out his accustomed role and expects Hendon to serve him, which he does. As a reward, Hendon is made a knight.

Shortly after, we learn that Henry VIII has died and Tom Canty is now king. As Tom rides in a grand procession through London, past Offal Court, he sees his mother and denies knowing her. Immediately he is stricken with remorse.

As the crown is about to be placed on Tom's head, Edward steps forward to protest. Before swapping places with Tom, he had hidden a seal in the palace and is able to say where, thereby establishing his true right to the throne. Tom Canty is made the King's Ward, and his sisters and his mother are granted lifetime care at Christ's Hospital.

Crossword 5
Modes of Travel in the Books of Mark Twain

Across

2 How Mark Twain travelled to Europe (9)

4 A common way for less wealthy people to travel (5)

7 How wealthy characters travel (8)

10 In *Tom Sawyer Abroad*, in Africa, Tom travels in a ... of camels (7)

11 Prominent symbol in *The Celebrated Jumping Frog of Calaveras County* (10)

13 Twain's description of travel in *Life on the Mississippi* (8)

14 Unusual means of transport in *Following the Equator* (8)

Down

1 Mode of transportation in *Roughing It* (10)

3 Primary means of travel in *A Connecticut Yankee in King Arthur's Court* (10)

5 Mark Twain's first job was on one of these (9)

6 How Huck and Jim travelled along the river (4)

8 Used by Twain to satirize society in *The Tragedy of Pudd'nhead Wilson* (9)

9 Pulled by mules in *The Adventures of Tom Sawyer* (4)

12 Tom Sawyer's favourite way of sailing down the river (5)

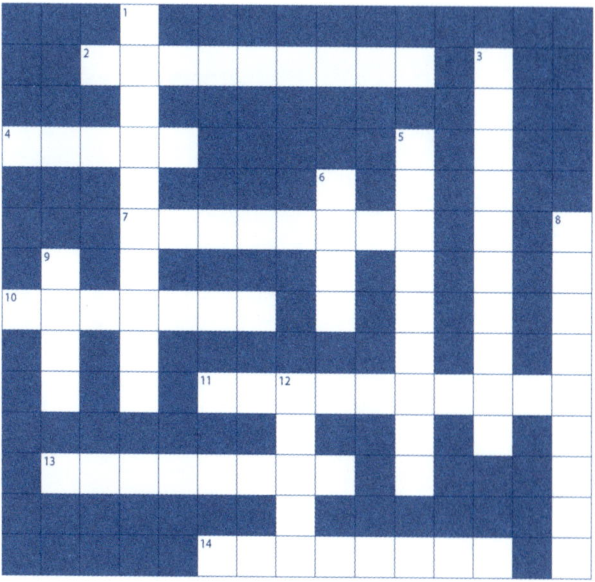

Cryptogram 5
Puddn'head Wilson's Calendar

In *The Tragedy of Puddn'head Wilson*, each chapter begins with an aphorism from 'Pudd'nhead Wilson's Calendar' – sayings collected by David Wilson, the narrator. Below is a cryptogram of one of those sayings. Each letter in the phrase has been replaced with a random number. See if you can unravel it.

A	B	C	D	E	F	G	H	I	J	K	L	M
						9	8					18

N	O	P	Q	R	S	T	U	V	W	X	Y	Z
24		13		21		6						

N		T	H		N	G			
24	20	6	8	2	24	9		12	20

N						R				R	M		N	G
12	3	3	22	12		21	3	23	20	21	18	2	24	9

				T	H		R		P			P			'
25	12		20	6	8	3	21		13	3	20	13	7	3	12

H				T	
8	25	4	2	6	12

Quiz 5
Fashion and Mark Twain

Mark Twain disliked the pompous language of society fashion magazines of the time and wrote a spoof fashion article in the 1860s for the *Territorial Enterprise*, Virginia, Nevada. He was, however, using authentic language to describe fashion at the time. What do the following words and phrases mean?

1 Burnous

2 Gimp

3 Guirpure

4 Pagoda cuffs

5 Garibaldi

6 Saute-en-barque

7 Foulard

8 Chenille

9 Magenta

10 Solferino

Wordsearch 6
Cats

Concealed in the grid on the facing page are sixteen of Mark Twain's inventive names for his cats. The names may read horizontally, vertically or diagonally, backwards or forwards, and letters may be used more than once, or not at all. Circle the answers on the grid and list them in the space below.

A	B	C	S	A	C	K	C	L	O	T	H	D	E	F
G	H	I	J	K	L	M	N	O	P	Q	R	S	T	U
V	W	X	Y	Z	Q	B	I	L	L	I	A	R	D	S
Z	N	A	P	O	L	L	I	N	A	R	I	S	S	P
Q	B	B	U	F	F	A	L	O	B	I	L	L	V	E
G	L	E	S	I	N	T	K	K	D	T	J	K	C	S
H	P	E	O	O	M	H	S	T	R	A	Y	K	I	T
V	Q	L	A	Z	U	E	F	S	L	M	A	I	D	I
T	P	Z	P	I	J	R	A	A	K	M	S	G	O	L
G	Z	E	Y	V	N	S	M	T	A	A	H	R	R	E
K	F	B	S	R	N	K	I	A	B	N	E	R	B	N
M	O	U	A	Q	A	I	N	N	S	Y	S	W	N	C
V	U	B	L	B	O	T	E	R	B	H	F	Q	J	E
Z	A	D	E	U	T	E	R	O	N	O	M	Y	S	L
W	E	V	E	Z	O	R	O	A	S	T	E	R	D	N

Picture Puzzle 6

Name the characters in the illustration below.

....

....

'Huckleberry was cordially hated and dreaded by all the mothers of the town because he was idle, and lawless, and vulgar, and bad – and because all their children admired him so, and delighted in his forbidden society, and wished they dared to be like him.'

The Adventures of Tom Sawyer

A Connecticut Yankee in King Arthur's Court (1889)

Hank Morgan, a nineteenth-century resident of Hartford, Connecticut, is transported back in time to the court of King Arthur at Camelot, after receiving a blow to the head. When Hank wakes up after the injury he doesn't know where he is and is accompanied by a knight to the court of King Arthur, which he believes to be some sort of insane asylum. Hank talks with a young man there, who tells him that the year is 528, and that the day is 19 June.

When Hank is told that he has been captured by the knight for a ransom, Hank uses his knowledge of modern science and technology to say that he is a magician more powerful than Merlin. Merlin is insulted and asks for proof. Hank realises from his knowledge of history that a solar eclipse will happen on 21 June and tells everyone that he will block out the sun. When the eclipse happens, he says that he will make the sun shine again. The eclipse fades and he becomes known as The Boss.

The story features many surreal time-travel moments with knights on bicycles and magicians using telephones, as Hank Morgan, The Boss, lives through many adventures with mythical historical figures. Hank Morgan never returns to nineteenth-century Connecticut and dies as The Boss in Camelot.

Crossword 6
Short Stories

Fill in the missing word in each case in the following titles of short stories by Mark Twain.

Across

4 A ... Story, Repeated Word for Word as I Heard It (4)
9 The ... White Elephant (6)
10 Cannibalism in the ... (4)
11 Mark Twain vs ... (7)
13 The ... Prayer (3)
14 The Story of the ... Little Boy (3)
15 The Canvasser's ... (4)
16 Is He ... or Is He Dead? (6)
17 The Million Pound Bank ... (4)
18 The Esquimau Maiden's ... (7)
19 A ... Nightmare (8)

Down

1 The Invalid's ... (5)
2 Some Learned ... for Good Old Boys and Girls (6)
3 Extract from Captain Stormfield's Visit to ... (6)

5 Those ... Twins (13)
6 My Late ... Secretaryship (10)
7 The Great ... in Pitcairn (10)
8 The Man That ... Hadleyburg (9)
12 A ... Barrelled Detective Story (6)

Wordsearch 7
Animals

Concealed in the grid on the facing page are the names of eighteen animals named in the novels of Mark Twain. The words may read horizontally, vertically or diagonally, backwards or forwards, and letters may be used more than once, or not at all. Circle the answers on the grid and list them in the space below.

O	F	A	B	C	D	E	F	G	H	I	J	L	K	L
M	R	N	O	P	Q	R	S	C	A	M	E	L	S	C
T	O	N	U	B	V	W	X	Y	R	R	Z	H	E	H
Y	G	R	I	A	X	T	G	P	E	O	P	F	A	A
L	S	W	H	T	M	W	M	K	O	C	W	W	S	M
R	G	U	Y	T	H	A	C	P	H	O	R	S	E	E
C	A	M	F	D	A	O	G	P	Q	Y	D	I	R	L
D	D	V	C	B	C	M	R	P	L	O	T	L	P	E
R	C	T	E	M	A	J	N	H	I	T	S	P	E	O
A	I	E	K	N	T	W	I	I	Y	E	J	B	N	N
K	J	Y	S	O	S	U	D	G	I	N	C	V	T	R
H	D	T	X	M	C	I	R	L	V	V	C	K	S	E
D	N	A	L	J	B	M	F	K	L	W	Y	H	P	S
A	H	Z	T	S	S	C	Y	I	E	N	O	G	U	C
E	G	P	D	Y	A	J	P	M	Q	Y	D	F	K	S

Picture Puzzle 7

Name the characters in the illustration below.

....

....

'Life is short. Break the rules. Forgive quickly. Kiss slowly. Love Truly. Laugh uncontrollably. Never regret anything that makes you smile.'

Mark Twain

The Tragedy of Pudd'nhead Wilson (1894)

David Wilson comes to Dawson's Landing in Missouri to begin a career as a lawyer. The southern townspeople dislike his northern wit and take him for an idiot, giving him the name Pudd'nhead. They refuse to give him their legal work, so he gets by doing odd jobs and spends most of his time pursuing his scientific hobbies, especially fingerprinting.

Roxana, or Roxy, is a beautiful woman, enslaved because she is one-sixteenth black, though she appears white. To save Chambers, her infant son, from a life of slavery, she switches him with Tom, the child of Mr Driscoll, her white master. Her son grows up as the heir to Mr Driscoll's estate, while Tom grows up as an enslaved man. When Mr Driscoll dies, he grants Roxy her freedom in his will. However, his heir, Tom Chambers, is a cruel, cowardly man, prone to drinking and gambling. His debts lead him to rob houses, sell Roxy (his biological mother) as a slave and murder his uncle, Judge Driscoll, in a botched robbery attempt.

Luigi and Angelo are twin showmen, wanting to settle down. They rent a room in Dawson's Landing, where Luigi catches Tom trying to steal a unique knife from him. They argue, Tom has Luigi arrested and Luigi accuses Tom of being a thief. Judge Driscoll, mortified, challenges Luigi to a duel. Tom tells his uncle that Luigi is a confessed assassin and therefore not an honourable man to duel.

Not long after, there is an election for mayor. Luigi, Angelo and Pudd'nhead stand as candidates. Because of the judge's claims against them, the twins lose and Pudd'nhead becomes the mayor.

Tom, badly in debt, murders the judge with the twins' knife while trying to rob him, then escapes. The twins, hearing the judge's cries, rush to help. They are found standing over the body, with their knife covered in blood. They stand trial for the murder and Pudd'nhead acts as their attorney. It is through his fingerprint collection that he not only discovers that Tom is the murderer, but that he is also really Chambers, Roxy's son. The twins are freed and Tom is thrown in jail.

Chambers is given back his place as Mr Driscoll's heir but struggles to fit in with society. Pudd'nhead is now the mayor and finally a successful lawyer, but he is without his old friends to enjoy his newfound success.

Pudd'nhead Wilson's calendar, quoted at the start of each chapter, captures his thoughts on his predicament.

Crossword 7
Adventures of Huckleberry Finn

Huck went on many adventures to different places using a variety of methods. Answer the travel-themed questions below to discover some of these locations.

Across

2 A moral compass for Huck's decisions (10)

5 Where Jim and Huck struggle with their conscience (12)

9 The main theme of the novel and the purpose of Huck's journey (7)

10 Huck and Jim's alternative mode of travel (5)

12 Where the Grangerfords wanted to move (8)

14 Huck and Jim's temporary home on Jackson's Island (3)

15 Where Huck and Jim first encounter the Duke and the King (8)

Down

1 Where Huck plays a prank on Jim when they first meet (16)

3 Where Huck hides the money he and Tom find in the cave (13)

4 The location of a sunken steamboat that Huck and Jim explore (13)

6 State which Huck and Jim plan to escape to (8)
7 Where Huck pretends to be Tom Sawyer and encounters Tom's real family (10)
8 Crop that Jim and Huck find on an abandoned boat (6)
11 Where Huck's adventures take him (7)
13 Last name of the family the Duke and King attempt to swindle (5)

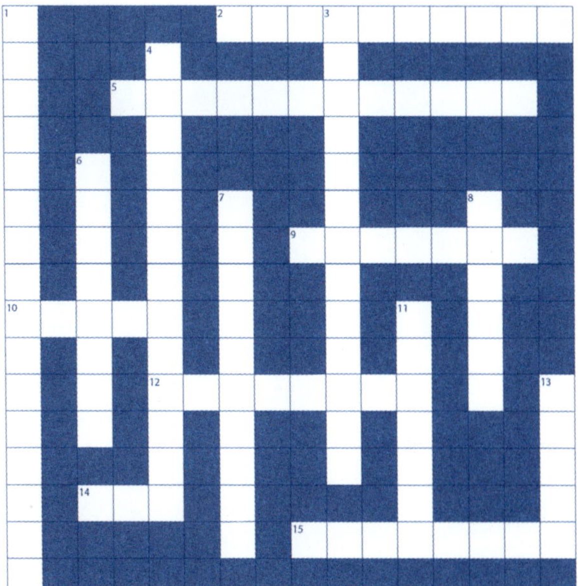

A Tramp Abroad (1880)

In this semi-autobiographical adventure through Europe, Mark Twain is the tramp, travelling with his friend, Harris. They are investigating life throughout eastern and southern Europe.

The novel explores Twain's adventures from Germany through Switzerland, France and Italy. This story intermixes Twain's real-life experiences with his creative imagination.

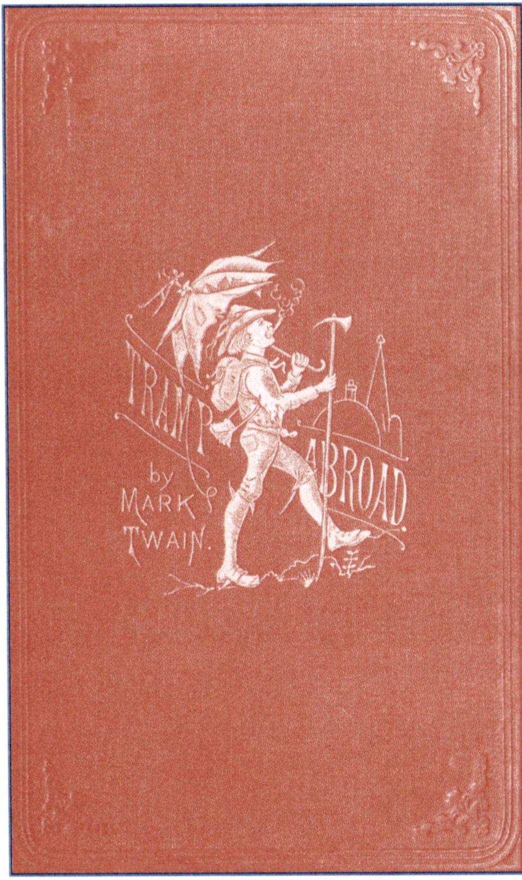
TRAMP
A
ABROAD
by
MARK
TWAIN.

Answers

Answers to pages 14–15

Wordsearch 1

Characters in *Adventures of Huckleberry Finn*

A	S	B	A	M	Y	L	A	W	R	E	N	C	E	P
C	D	I	E	F	T	O	M	S	A	W	Y	E	R	U
G	H	I	L	J	K	L	M	N	O	L	P	R	Q	D
J	O	E	H	A	R	P	E	R	L	R	E	S	T	D
U	V	W	X	Y	S	Z	V	O	K	Y	L	G	S	N
C	J	E	N	S	L	P	P	T	W	P	F	H	D	H
B	B	E	C	K	Y	T	H	A	T	C	H	E	R	E
K	V	F	R	E	N	S	S	E	A	K	W	B	R	A
J	X	K	Q	U	V	D	I	F	L	Y	K	U	O	D
W	H	Z	A	G	I	J	A	F	Q	P	S	A	B	W
T	P	A	P	S	F	I	N	N	J	R	S	Z	I	I
R	V	C	P	A	D	K	B	J	Q	J	T	L	N	L
U	W	X	C	O	M	R	D	O	B	B	I	N	S	S
M	U	F	F	P	O	T	T	E	R	Q	U	M	O	O
H	U	C	K	L	E	B	E	R	R	Y	F	I	N	N

Answers to pages 16–17

Name Game I

injunjoe
mrdobbins
muffpotter
huckleberryfinn
mary
sidneysawyer
auntpolly
judgethatcher
alfredtemple

Answers to page 18

Picture Puzzle 1

Tom Sawyer

Aunt Polly

Mary

Answers to page 19

First to Last

1 *The Adventures of Tom Sawyer* (1876)

2 *The Annotated Huckleberry Finn* (1884)

3 *Adventures of Huckleberry Finn* (1884)

4 *Tom Sawyer Abroad* (1894)

5 *Tom Sawyer, Detective* (1896)

Answers to pages 22–3

(answers to pages 22–3)

Crossword I

Characters in *Adventures of Huckleberry Finn*

Answers to page 24

Cryptogram 1
Puddn'head Wilson's Calendar

A	B	C	D	E	F	G	H	I	J	K	L	M
16	11	20	10	26	14	17	18	1	21	19	7	22

N	O	P	Q	R	S	T	U	V	W	X	Y	Z
25	4	9	12	15	23	24	3	13	6	2	25	8

M A N   M A Y   H A V E
22 16 25   22 16 5   18 16 13 26

N O   B A D   H A B I T S
25 4   11 16 10   18 16 11 1 24 23

A N D   H A V E   W O R S E
16 25 10   18 16 13 26   6 4 15 23 26

Answers to page 25

Quiz I
Relations in Mark Twain's Novels

1 Sid Sawyer

2 Pap Finn

3 Sally Phelps

4 Judge Thatcher

5 Percy Driscoll

6 Roxanna ('Roxy')

7 Sally 'Gwendoline' Sellers

8 Luigi Capello

9 Silas Phelps

10 King Henry VIII

Answers to pages 26–7

True or False?

1 The answer is b. Some sources credit Oscar Wilde, but variations of this sentiment have been noted as far back as the fourteenth century, suggesting that the inventor of this proverb will remain forever unknown. a) From *The Innocents Abroad*; c) From a letter to D. W. Bowser, 20 March 1880; d) From *A Tramp Abroad.*

2 The answer is b. American author, H. Jackson Brown attributed it to his mother in his book *P.S. I Love You: When Mom Wrote, She Always Saved the Best for Last* (1991). a) From *Eruption*; c) Notebook, 1904; d) From *A Tramp Abroad.*

3 The answer is a. This quote has also been attributed to Lincoln, Franklin and even Galileo, so the source cannot be verified. b) Notebook, 1894; c) *Disappearance of Literature* (speech); d) Notebook, 1894.

4 The answer is a. It was actually Blaise Pascal, a French physicist and writer. b) From *Taming the Bicycle*; c) *Autobiography of Mark Twain*; d) From *What is Man?*

5 The answer is c. James M. Barrie, writer and creator of *Peter Pan*, used similar phrases in the 1890s. However, accounts show that politician Ben Wade said something nearly identical in the 1880s. a) *From The Tragedy of Pudd'nhead Wilson*; b) From 'Hellfire Hotchkiss', *Satires and Burlesques*; d) From 'Advice to Youth'.

Answers to pages 28–9

Wordsearch 2

Places in *A Tramp Abroad*

A B C D E F G G H I J K E L M
N O P Z Q R S T E U V C T W X
B A D E N B A D E N I S Y Z C
I B D R L U C E R N E K K I Q
T B L M R K Z Q E R N V M N C
A O I A Q H Y V O Y N H A T I
O O Z T G W K F G G T Q N E F
X E Y T F D K R J X E A N R W
J F B N W C X A I V L R H L R
K E K O A W B N V I B U E A U
P G D L S X O C M W W D I K J
J K B E P M U E R X R O M E D
N E C K A R R I V E R N A N D
J A S H E I D E L B E R G O V
O G C R A C D E J O O P F M E

Answers to pages 30–1

Name Game 2

humphreymar**l**ow
j**o**hncanty
ladyma**r**y
la**d**yelizabeth
mot**h**ercanty
b**e**thcanty
ladyjaneg**r**ey
tomcan**t**y
fatherandrew
hug**o**
blakeand**r**ews
mileshan**d**on

Answers to page 32

Picture Puzzle 2

Tom Sawyer

Mr Dobbins

Becky Thatcher

Amy Lawrence

Answers to pages 36–7

Crossword 2

The Life of Mark Twain

Answers to page 38

Cryptogram 2

Puddn'head Wilson's Calendar

A	B	C	D	E	F	G	H	I	J	K	L	M
14	5	2	21	24	3	18	1	9	22	20	11	7

N	O	P	Q	R	S	T	U	V	W	X	Y	Z
15	8	25	26	10	13	23	6	19	12	16	4	17

W	H	E	N		A	N	G	R	Y		C	O	U	N	T
12	1	24	15		14	15	18	10	4		2	8	6	15	23

F	O	U	R		W	H	E	N		V	E	R	HY
3	8	6	10		12	1	24	15		19	24	10	4

A	N	G	R	Y		S	W	E	A	R
14	15	18	10	4		13	12	24	14	10

Answers to page 39

Quiz 2
Places in the Novels of Mark Twain

1 St Petersburg, Missouri

2 The gates of the Palace of Westminster, London

3 Dawson's Landing

4 Offal Court, London

5 Jackson's Island in the Mississippi River

6 The Court of King Arthur, England

7 Cholmondeley Castle, Warwickshire, England

8 Yale University

9 The Mississippi

10 Africa

Answers to pages 40–41

Wordsearch 3

Food in *A Tramp Abroad*

A	B	B	C	D	C	L	A	M	S	E	F	G	T	H
I	J	L	K	L	M	N	R	A	D	I	S	H	E	S
O	O	A	P	Q	C	A	C	P	R	S	T	U	R	H
V	Y	C	W	X	R	P	R	L	Y	Z	I	S	R	E
Q	S	K	R	S	A	P	O	E	Y	S	C	N	A	E
L	T	B	P	A	N	L	A	S	O	O	W	W	P	P
T	E	A	Q	P	B	E	K	Y	R	K	N	O	I	S
J	R	S	T	O	E	S	E	R	U	I	W	O	N	H
X	S	S	R	S	R	K	R	U	T	V	M	D	G	E
K	M	P	O	S	R	E	S	P	Y	S	H	C	I	A
O	M	V	U	U	I	C	S	S	D	Q	B	O	V	D
Z	J	K	T	M	E	B	E	Q	N	L	F	C	P	L
V	X	W	L	L	S	R	A	C	H	I	C	K	E	N
V	K	P	V	O	K	B	U	C	K	W	H	E	A	T
P	A	R	T	R	I	D	G	E	S	C	F	O	K	Q

Answers to pages 42–3

Name Game 3

tomsa**w**yer
papf**i**nn
jakepackar**d**
mrswats**o**n
tomsa**w**yer
buckgrangerfor**d**
drr**o**binson
h**u**ckleberryfinn
jud**g**ethatcher
peterwi**l**ks
tommyb**a**rnes
colonel**s**herburn

Answers to page 44

Picture Puzzle 3

Billy Fisher

Tom Sawyer

Mary

Sid Sawyer

Answers to pages 48–9

Crossword 3

The Adventures of Tom Sawyer

Answers to page 50

Cryptogram 3

Puddn'head Wilson's Calendar

A	B	C	D	E	F	G	H	I	J	K	L	M
19	1	11	26	3	16	4	6	2	8	9	14	17

N	O	P	Q	R	S	T	U	V	W	X	Y	Z
20	5	10	25	21	15	12	23	7	16	22	13	24

W H E N   I L L   L U C K
16 6 3 20   2 14 14   14 23 11 9

B E G I N S   I T   D O E S   N O T
1 3 4 2 20 15   2 12   26 5 3 15   20 5 12

C O M E   I N   S P R I N K L E S
11 5 17 23   2 20   15 10 21 2 20 9 14 3 15

B U T   I N   S H O W E R S
1 23 12   2 20   15 6 5 16 3 21 15

Answers to page 51

Quiz 3

Crime in Mark Twain's Novels

1 Stolen gold

2 Injun Joe

3 By pretending to be his brothers Harvey and William Wilks

4 Highway robbery

5 He stages his cabin as if someone has broken in and killed him, leaving his body in the river

6 He was shot in the back

7 Buck Grangerford

8 Into Peter Wilks' coffin

9 Muff Potter

10 Grave robbery

Answers to pages 52–3

Wordsearch 4

Fish and Amphibians in the Writing of Mark Twain

M U S K E L L U N G E A B B C
D E F G H I J K L T M N L O P
Q R S T S U W V U W X Y U Z P
L L D M Z R A O G U W K E S A
B B A R N T R M H B H Z G T D
W L S W S T M E G S O B I U D
C A U F H A O X I V T U L R L
C B L E O I U F P X U L L G E
L N Y L B E T G O C R L S E F
E T H D E A H E E C T F T O I
E Y M P C Y S Y B R L R C N S
C R A P P I E S B A E O T T H
P R C O M U S S E L S G Z G N
I X G R E E N F R O G S P S E
Z Z N S J F K C H R P B M J H

Answers to page 54

Picture Puzzle 4

Tom Sawyer

Ben Rogers

Answers to pages 58–9

Crossword 4

Mark Twain's Humour

Answers to page 60

Cryptogram 4

Puddn'head Wilson's Calendar

A	B	C	D	E	F	G	H	I	J	K	L	M
6	15	22	16	1	7	23	2	11	17	12	4	18

N	O	P	Q	R	S	T	U	V	W	X	Y	Z
13	14	9	8	21	24	25	10	26	5	20	3	19

C O U R A G E   I S
22 14 10 21 6 23 1   11 24

R E S I S T A N C E   T O   F E A R
21 1 24 11 24 25 6 13 22 1   25 14   7 1 6 21

M A S T E R Y   O F   F E A R   N O T
18 6 24 25 1 21 3   14 7   7 1 6 21   13 14 25

A B S E N C E   O F   F E A R
6 15 24 1 13 22 1   14 7   7 1 6 21

Answers to page 61

Quiz 4

Dialect in the Novels of Mark Twain

1 Going

2 A large barrel used to transport gallons of sugar by ship

3 A simpleton or stupid person

4 A person who pretends to be sophisticated or thinks too highly of themselves

5 An eighteenth-century term for a wealthy, highly educated, powerful and influential person

6 Consequences

7 A nineteenth-century colloquialism for sneak thieves or pickpockets

8 Elocution

9 Nineteenth-century term meaning to steal, pilfer or acquire illegally

10 A musical instrument, dating back to as early as the sixteenth century

11 Anonymous

12 The Tuileries

13 Brother

Answers to pages 62–3

Wordsearch 5

Themes

M O R A L I T Y A L B C D E F
G O H I J K L M E N O P Q H R
S T N U V W X V Y Z A I Q Y X
R J R E F L A S L N C F N P F
F P Q X Y R A W O N I B A O R
R Q S J T J I U E C V X S C E
Q Z S D W A E E J A I A W R E
L H A Q L D D D N F L E O I D
S N M L H C J V U D I T T S O
S O M A X J Q U E C S G H Y M
O X L Y U M V C S N A H R W P
T M T M K O O K D T T T I R W
H M L O H E Q V L Q I U I P F
E T D F M J T T Q V O C R O Q
V N Q Y B C L J Z M N P E E N

Answers to page 64

Picture Puzzle 5

Joe Harper

Ben Rogers

Huckleberry Finn

Tom Sawyer

Tommy Barnes

Answers to pages 68–9

Crossword 5

Modes of Travel in the Books of Mark Twain

Answers to page 70

Cryptogram 5

Puddn'head Wilson's Calendar

A	B	C	D	E	F	G	H	I	J	K	L	M
25	4	10	22	3	23	9	8	2	19	5	7	18

N	O	P	Q	R	S	T	U	V	W	X	Y	Z
24	20	13	11	21	12	6	14	26	1	16	17	15

N O T H I N G   S O
24 20 6 8 2 24 9   12 20

N E E D S   R E F O R M I N G
12 3 3 22 12   21 3 23 20 21 18 2 24 9

A S   O T H E R   P E O P L E ' S
25 12   20 6 8 3 21   13 3 20 13 7 3 12

H A B I T S
8 25 4 2 6 12

Answers to page 71

Quiz 5
Fashion and Mark Twain

1 A cape with a bobble-tipped hood, usually worn by women as an evening cloak

2 Twisted silk, worsted or cotton with a cord or wire running through it, used chiefly as trimming

3 A heavy lace consisting of embroidered motifs held together by large connecting stitches

4 Flared sleeves that stop mid-forearm to reveal sleeves underneath and thus a tiered effect

5 A voluminous blouse of the colour red worn by supporters of Garibaldi, very popular in 1862

6 A flared three-quarter-length coat without sleeves worn with a matching skirt

7 A thin, soft material of silk or silk and cotton, often with a printed pattern

8 A tufted velvety cord or yarn, used for trimming furniture and making carpets and clothing

9 One of the first synthetic dyes, a brilliant purple-red, derived from coal tar

10 A purplish-red colour named after the Battle of Solferino, in Italy, which came into favour in 1859. Mark Twain even used the word to describe facial hair

Answers to pages 72–3

Wordsearch 6

Cats

A	B	C	S	A	C	K	C	L	O	T	H	D	E	F
G	H	I	J	K	L	M	N	O	P	Q	R	S	T	U
V	W	X	Y	Z	Q	B	I	L	L	I	A	R	D	S
Z	N	A	P	O	L	L	I	N	A	R	I	S	S	P
Q	B	B	U	F	F	A	L	O	B	I	L	L	V	E
G	L	E	S	I	N	T	K	K	D	T	J	K	C	S
H	P	E	O	O	M	H	S	T	R	A	Y	K	I	T
V	Q	L	A	Z	U	E	F	S	L	M	A	I	D	I
T	P	Z	P	I	J	R	A	A	K	M	S	G	O	L
G	Z	E	Y	V	N	S	M	T	A	A	H	R	R	E
K	F	B	S	R	N	K	I	A	B	N	E	R	B	N
M	O	U	A	Q	A	I	N	N	S	Y	S	W	N	C
V	U	B	L	B	O	T	E	R	B	H	F	Q	J	E
Z	A	D	E	U	T	E	R	O	N	O	M	Y	S	L
W	E	V	E	Z	O	R	O	A	S	T	E	R	D	N

Answers to page 74

Picture Puzzle 6

Widow Douglas

Huckleberry Finn

Answers to pages 78–9

Crossword 6

Short Stories

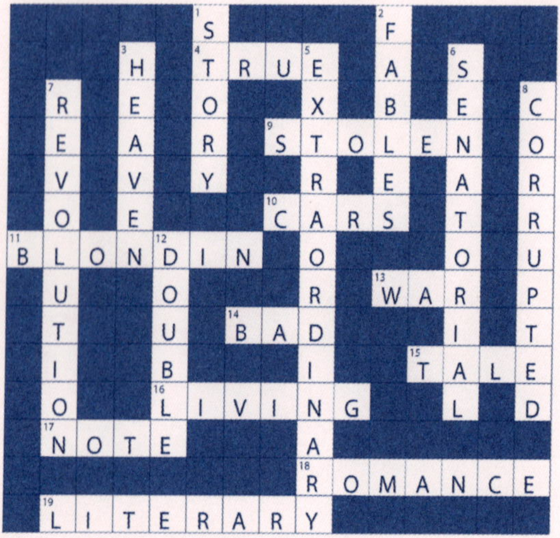

Answers to pages 80–81

Wordsearch 7

Animals

O	F	A	B	C	D	E	F	G	H	I	J	L	K	L
M	R	N	O	P	Q	R	S	C	A	M	E	L	S	C
T	O	N	U	B	V	W	X	Y	R	R	Z	H	E	H
Y	G	R	I	A	X	T	G	P	E	O	P	F	A	A
L	S	W	H	T	M	W	M	K	O	C	W	W	S	M
R	G	U	Y	T	H	A	C	P	H	O	R	S	E	E
C	A	M	F	D	A	O	G	P	Q	Y	D	I	R	L
D	D	V	C	B	C	M	R	P	L	O	T	L	P	E
R	C	T	E	M	A	J	N	H	I	T	S	P	E	O
A	I	E	K	N	T	W	I	I	Y	E	J	B	N	N
K	J	Y	S	O	S	U	D	G	I	N	C	V	T	R
H	D	T	X	M	C	I	R	L	V	V	C	K	S	E
D	N	A	L	J	B	M	F	K	L	W	Y	H	P	S
A	H	Z	T	S	S	C	Y	I	E	N	O	G	U	C
E	G	P	D	Y	A	J	P	M	Q	Y	D	F	K	S

Answers to page 82

Picture Puzzle 7

Charlotte Grangerford

Sophie Grangerford

Answers to pages 86–7

Crossword 7

Adventures of Huckleberry Finn

Picture Credits

Shutterstock: T. Gorhum, 3; Naci Yavuz, 4; Real_life_photo, 88. Wikimedia Commons: E. W. Kemble, 7, 35; A. F. Bradley, 11; G. H. Jones, 12; Achille-Louis-Joseph Sirouy, 32, 82; Paramount Pictures, 42; Sodacan, 67; Howard Pyle, 77; 89; ArtMari, 90. thegraphicsfairy.com: 16, 19, 21, 30, 62, 71. True Williams: 18, 44, 47, 54, 57. Freepik: rawpixel.com, 28, 40, 52, 61, 80. E. W. Kemble: 64, 74. Diane Law: 72.